THE BOXCAR CHILDREN MYSTERIES

...SE ISLAND
...OW HOUSE MYSTERY
...RANCH
...STERY
...MYSTERY
...SHED MYSTERY
...THOUSE MYSTERY
...N TOP MYSTERY
...HOUSE MYSTERY
...SE MYSTERY
...SEBOAT MYSTERY
...OWBOUND MYSTERY
...REE HOUSE MYSTERY
BICYCLE MYSTERY
MYSTERY IN THE SAND
MYSTERY BEHIND THE WALL
BUS STATION MYSTERY
BENNY UNCOVERS A MYSTERY
THE HAUNTED CABIN MYSTERY
THE DESERTED LIBRARY MYSTERY
THE ANIMAL SHELTER MYSTERY
THE OLD MOTEL MYSTERY
THE MYSTERY OF THE HIDDEN PAINTING
THE AMUSEMENT PARK MYSTERY
THE MYSTERY OF THE MIXED-UP ZOO
THE CAMP-OUT MYSTERY
THE MYSTERY GIRL
THE MYSTERY CRUISE
THE DISAPPEARING FRIEND MYSTERY
THE MYSTERY OF THE SINGING GHOST
THE MYSTERY IN THE SNOW
THE PIZZA MYSTERY
THE MYSTERY HORSE
THE MYSTERY AT THE DOG SHOW
THE CASTLE MYSTERY
THE MYSTERY OF THE LOST VILLAGE
THE MYSTERY ON THE ICE
THE MYSTERY OF THE PURPLE POOL
THE GHOST SHIP MYSTERY
THE MYSTERY IN WASHINGTON, DC
THE CANOE TRIP MYSTERY
THE MYSTERY OF THE HIDDEN BEACH
THE MYSTERY OF THE MISSING CAT
THE MYSTERY AT SNOWFLAKE INN

THE MYSTERY ON STAGE
THE DINOSAUR MYSTERY
THE MYSTERY OF THE STOLEN MUSIC
THE MYSTERY AT THE BALL PARK
THE CHOCOLATE SUNDAE MYSTERY
THE MYSTERY OF THE HOT AIR BALLOON
THE MYSTERY BOOKSTORE
THE PILGRIM VILLAGE MYSTERY
THE MYSTERY OF THE STOLEN BOXCAR
THE MYSTERY IN THE CAVE
THE MYSTERY ON THE TRAIN
THE MYSTERY AT THE FAIR
THE MYSTERY OF THE LOST MINE
THE GUIDE DOG MYSTERY
THE HURRICANE MYSTERY
THE PET SHOP MYSTERY
THE MYSTERY OF THE SECRET MESSAGE
THE FIREHOUSE MYSTERY
THE MYSTERY IN SAN FRANCISCO
THE NIAGARA FALLS MYSTERY
THE MYSTERY AT THE ALAMO
THE OUTER SPACE MYSTERY
THE SOCCER MYSTERY
THE MYSTERY IN THE OLD ATTIC
THE GROWLING BEAR MYSTERY
THE MYSTERY OF THE LAKE MONSTER
THE MYSTERY AT PEACOCK HALL
THE WINDY CITY MYSTERY
THE BLACK PEARL MYSTERY
THE CEREAL BOX MYSTERY
THE PANTHER MYSTERY
THE MYSTERY OF THE QUEEN'S JEWELS
THE STOLEN SWORD MYSTERY
THE BASKETBALL MYSTERY
THE MOVIE STAR MYSTERY
THE MYSTERY OF THE PIRATE'S MAP
THE GHOST TOWN MYSTERY
THE MYSTERY OF THE BLACK RAVEN
THE MYSTERY IN THE MALL
THE MYSTERY IN NEW YORK
THE GYMNASTICS MYSTERY
THE POISON FROG MYSTERY
THE MYSTERY OF THE EMPTY SAFE
THE HOME RUN MYSTERY
THE GREAT BICYCLE RACE MYSTERY

P9-BIG-036

THE BOXCAR CHILDREN®

CREATED BY
GERTRUDE CHANDLER WARNER

BOOK

152

SECRET ON THE THIRTEENTH FLOOR

ILLUSTRATED BY
ANTHONY VanARSDALE

ALBERT WHITMAN & COMPANY
CHICAGO, ILLINOIS

Contents

A Good Coincidence

It was a sunny day in early May. The trees were alive with birdsong, and the Alden children were hard at work in their front yard. Henry raked grass clippings into a large pile in the middle of the lawn. Then he tilted down a garbage can so his younger brother, Benny, could scoop them inside.

Near the front steps, Violet wore a pair of purple gardening gloves and used a spade to dig a row of evenly spaced holes in the dark soil of the garden beds. Her sister, Jessie, carried trays of flowers from their grandfather's car around to the front of the house, carefully stepping around their dog, Watch, who lay snoozing in the sun. The plastic containers held snapdragons, geraniums, and pansies.

"I just love spring," Violet said as she wiped a spot of dirt off her cheek with her forearm. She gazed at the collection of peach, red, yellow, pink, and white blossoms.

"Me too!" Jessie said. "It's the most colorful season—that's for sure."

"I love getting outside after being cooped up all winter," Henry added. As the oldest of the Alden children, at fourteen, he was getting stronger every month, and Grandfather appreciated his help with all the outdoor chores.

The Aldens hadn't always spent their days this way. After their parents died in a car accident, the four children were supposed to go live with their grandfather right away. But they had been afraid he would be mean and that they wouldn't like living with him. So instead, Henry, Jessie, Violet, and Benny had run away to the woods, where they'd found an abandoned boxcar and made it into a home. They'd discovered Watch in the woods too and had made him part of their family.

When Grandfather Alden found them, the

children realized he was not mean at all! They were excited to move into the house he lived in with his housekeeper, Mrs. McGregor. Of course, Watch came along too, and Grandfather Alden set the boxcar up in his backyard for the children to use as a playhouse. Now they loved living in a neighborhood.

Back in the front yard, Benny suddenly leaped to the side and sent his armload of grass clippings fluttering back down to the lawn. He covered his face and then peeked out through his fingers at something buzzing near his head. "Bees are the only bad news about spring," he said.

"Don't bother that bee, and he won't bother you," Jessie said. She was twelve and very sensible about things that worried some children, especially Benny. "Pollinators are a very important part of the ecosystem," she added. "If we didn't have bees, we wouldn't have honey."

"Not only that," Henry added, "but seeing bees is a sign. Mrs. McGregor learned that from her aunt in Ireland. When you see bees buzzing around your house or near your windows, it means a visitor will soon arrive. And you should

never try to kill the bee, because that means the visitor will bring bad news."

Benny thought this over while he stood very still, watching the black-and-yellow creature zoom past his face. He didn't like the idea of the bee being a sign. Soon the buzzing stopped. He waited another moment to be sure the bee was gone and then used the rake to gather the fallen clippings. The work seemed to go fast when he thought about good things—like the famous honey cake Mrs. McGregor liked to make in the summer.

"Is anybody else getting hungry?" Benny asked.

Henry smiled and looked at his watch. "It *is* almost lunchtime," he said. "Maybe we should head inside and wash up."

Just as he was leaning the rake up against the front porch, a white van pulled up in front of their house.

Benny's eyes went wide, and he looked at Henry. At the same time, they both said, "A visitor!"

"Hello, children!" called Ms. Singleton, getting out of the van. Ms. Singleton was the mail carrier assigned to the Aldens' neighborhood. Like most mail carriers, she wore navy blue shorts, but on her feet were bright-pink hiking boots. She also wore a pink scarf tied inside the collar of her blue work shirt.

"You are earning your keep today, I see," Ms. Singleton said when she saw all the work the Aldens had done on the yard.

"We don't mind," Jessie said. "Especially on such a beautiful day."

Ms. Singleton shuffled through a pile of mail she held under her arm and pulled out a catalog and two letters. "Not too much today," she said, then tapped the letter on top. "But this one looks pretty official."

Jessie took the mail. The return address on the letter said COUNTY COURTHOUSE, and there was an official-looking seal stamped below marked URGENT. "We were just about to go inside for lunch," she said. "We'll make sure Grandfather sees this."

"You picked a good time to go inside," Ms. Singleton said, pointing to the eastern sky. An enormous gray cloud was moving in. Soon it would cover the sun and bring a soaking spring rain. "I'd say that's a bad sign."

"Yikes!" Henry said. "Might be a good afternoon for reading a book."

The children waved good-bye to Ms. Singleton. "I wonder why she said that the cloud was a bad sign," Violet said. "A cloud is just a cloud...isn't it?"

Inside, Jessie ran straight to Grandfather's study, with the letter in her hand. Seeing the words about the courthouse had made her nervous. "This just came for you, Grandfather," Jessie said. "You aren't in trouble, are you?"

Grandfather took the letter and chuckled. "I sure hope not," he said. "How about I open it at the table?"

He and the children washed up for lunch, and Mrs. McGregor carried a platter of turkey sandwiches and a fruit salad to the table. Henry poured lemonade, and they all sat down.

Grandfather put on his reading glasses, opened the envelope, and scanned the letter. After a moment, he grinned. "Well, would you look at that."

"It's not trouble, then?" Jessie asked.

Grandfather shook his head. "Nothing to worry

about, but it *is* important. This is an official jury summons."

"What's that?" Violet asked.

Grandfather took off his glasses. "Every citizen in our country who is over the age of eighteen has a responsibility to serve on a jury when he or she is called. A jury is just a group of regular people who play an important role in court cases. They listen to the facts and make a decision about whether someone who has been accused of a crime is guilty."

"Wow," Henry said. "That sounds like a big job."

"It can be," Grandfather said. "But I have never done it before. Even as old as I am, I've never been called for jury duty. My friend Sam, on the other hand—that young man who owns the car wash downtown—he just told me last week that he's been called five different times!"

Violet popped a strawberry into her mouth. "Why do they keep calling him instead of you?" she asked.

"They aren't doing it on purpose," Grandfather said. "People are chosen for jury duty at random. So it's just a coincidence that he has been called so many times."

Benny's forehead wrinkled, and he twisted up his mouth. Jessie could tell that he was confused.

"Benny," Jessie said, "a coincidence means something that happens by chance, not for any reason. The people in charge didn't call Sam so many times on purpose."

"Hmm," Benny said. "Well, either way, jury duty sounds pretty boring if you have to sit in a room and listen to a lot of people talk. Unless they have snacks."

Grandfather laughed. "Actually, they do sometimes, if the case goes on a long time. The judge makes sure the jury gets to take breaks for meals, and sometimes they even order food for the jurors to eat if they can't leave the courthouse."

"Like pizza?" Benny asked, his eyes brightening.

"Probably," Grandfather said. "But even without pizza, I am happy to do my duty now that it's my turn. I have to go to Silver City to do it."

"I love Silver City!" Jessie said.

"Yes, me too," said Grandfather, "and come to think of it, this jury summons might be a *good* coincidence. I've been looking for an opportunity to get to Silver City to visit my friend Gwen. We went to high school together, but I haven't seen her in years. She has been going through a bad few months. This could be excellent timing."

Violet looked concerned. "What happened to her?"

"There was a fire in the apartment building Gwen owns—the Bixby," Grandfather said. "Fortunately, no one got hurt. But the building was damaged. It's almost one hundred years old, and it's built in a style called art deco, which was popular in the 1920s."

"What's art deco?" Henry asked, taking the last bite of his sandwich.

"That means the design contains all kinds of interesting decoration," Grandfather said, "like silver and gold and tiles in bright patterns. The whole building is a work of art. It's going to take a lot of careful work to bring it all back to the way it used to be."

"Maybe we could help," Henry said.

Grandfather thought this over. "I'm not sure," he said. "That kind of work can be really difficult.

Lots of dirt. Lots of heavy lifting."

"But Grandfather, you saw how much work we did in the front yard today," Jessie said.

"That's right," Henry added. "The Aldens don't shy away from hard work. I think we could handle this job. And don't forget, school is closed on Monday and Tuesday."

Grandfather smiled. "You know, you're right. I would love to introduce you to Gwen, and she sure could use a few extra sets of hands. Let's take a long weekend in Silver City."

Violet clapped her hands. She remembered that she had a book in her room about architecture. She wanted to look in the index to see if it said anything about the art deco style Grandfather had described. It sounded beautiful.

Just then, a large clap of thunder interrupted the conversation, and fat drops began to plink against the window.

"Oh no," Benny said. "The bad sign! Just like Ms. Singleton said."

"Or," Henry said, "it is just a coincidence."

The Curse

On Saturday, Grandfather drove carefully through dense traffic into Silver City. He tried not to honk his horn too many times before he finally reached their destination and pulled into the driveway of the Bixby building. The Aldens got out and looked up at the slender structure, crowned at the top with a faded copper roof. The newer steel and glass buildings that surrounded it gleamed in the sun. In comparison, the Bixby's small, antique windows and faded stone walls looked a little tired. Jessie noticed that some windows on the top floor were blackened with soot. That must have been where the fire had taken place.

Grandfather and Henry grabbed the suitcases

out of the trunk, and the Aldens went together into the lobby. It took a moment for their eyes to adjust from the bright sunshine to the dim space, which was lit by old-fashioned lamps. Violet was the first to notice the floor.

"Look!" she said, crouching down to touch the tiles with her fingers. Tiny triangles and squares of different colors had been arranged into an abstract design. Violet had enjoyed learning about the ideas behind art deco design in her book at home. The artists and architects who embraced this style believed in using fine materials like ivory and colored glass. They wanted their designs to showcase beautiful work. "Don't you love how these colors and shapes look?" she said.

Benny shook his head. To him, the triangles didn't make a pretty pattern. Instead, they reminded him of something scary, like a monster's teeth, and the gloomy room didn't help. "I don't know," he said. "I think they're spooky."

Grandfather patted Benny on the shoulder. "Oh no, Benny," he said. "There's nothing spooky about this old place."

Just then the door behind the front desk opened and out stepped a woman with spiky silver hair and red glasses. She had a big, friendly smile.

"I thought I heard someone come in!" she said.

She crossed the lobby, and Grandfather gave her a hug. "You haven't changed a bit," he said.

"Well, aren't you kind?" the woman said. Then she pointed to her head. "But I don't think I had gray hair back when we were teenagers."

"Children, this is my friend Gwen," Grandfather said.

The Aldens introduced themselves, and Gwen shook hands with each of them.

Benny noticed the fireplace in the lobby was partly covered up with plywood. "Did something break?" he asked Gwen.

"Oh," Gwen said with a sigh, "that was just the first of many problems we've had around here. The marble tiles on the fireplace have cracks and are starting to fall apart. A chunk of marble fell when one of our former tenants was standing here, and it nearly broke his toe! He moved out the next week."

Benny's eyes got very big, and he took a large step away from the fireplace.

Gwen led them down a narrow hallway that Benny thought seemed even gloomier than the lobby. He leaned close to Jessie, so no one else could hear him. "This place is spooky," he whispered. Jessie squeezed his hand.

"People say they love the historical details of this old building," Gwen was saying to Grandfather as they came to the elevators. "But I just don't know. Even before the fire, we were having trouble renting out units on the thirteenth floor. It's silly, but people say it's cursed. Now thirteen has so much damage, we have to redo the entire floor. And there are so many new buildings around now. I'm afraid people would rather live in those instead. They have all the new features, like dishwashers and air conditioners and big, bright windows."

Violet thought this over as she looked at the elevators. Even they had fancy decorations. The doors were brass, and above them, a half-moon-shaped dial showed the numbers for the floors. On the dial, an arrow moved as the elevator went from floor to floor, sort of like the hand on a clock. "Those new buildings might be nice," Violet said, "but they're also a little boring, don't you think? This place is one of a kind."

Gwen put her hand on Violet's shoulder. She looked at Grandfather and grinned. "You told me your grandchildren are special, and you were right," she said.

"Why do people say the thirteenth floor is cursed?" Benny asked. He sounded worried.

Grandfather waved his hand. "That's just something people say. Traditionally, thirteen is said to be the most unlucky number of all," he said. "But thirteen is just a number, like any other number. There's nothing spooky about it."

They stood waiting for the old elevator and watched the half-moon dial as the arrow made its way to the L for lobby. When the door opened, a tall woman wearing bright-coral lipstick and big black sunglasses walked out. She was using a cane, which made a clicking sound on the tile floor. When the woman saw Gwen standing there, she stopped and put her hand on her hip. "There you are. I've been looking all over for you. You *must* do something about the construction noise on the thirteenth floor. I've been listening to the pounding through my ceiling all morning."

The elevator doors closed again with everyone still in the hallway. Gwen looked uneasy. "Mrs. Mason, these are my friends, the Aldens. They are here visiting from Greenfield."

The children smiled at Mrs. Mason and said hello. She raised her sunglasses to the top of her head, but she did not smile back. Instead, she narrowed her eyes. She turned back to Gwen. "I do not want a bunch of children running around and making noise," Mrs. Mason said. "What I want is some peace and quiet!"

"I'm very sorry the noise has been bothering you," Gwen said. "I will make sure the workers finish up by dinnertime."

"See that you do," Mrs. Mason said. Then she stormed off.

Gwen had to push the button to call the elevator again, and after a moment, its doors opened. Gwen and the Aldens stepped inside, and everyone was quiet. Violet looked concerned. "I think we got off on the wrong foot with Mrs. Mason," she said.

Gwen shook her head. "Most days, I think there is no right foot with Mrs. Mason. She was very good friends with Sam, the former owner of the Bixby, and she has never gotten over him selling the building to me."

When the elevator reached the twelfth floor, the bell dinged, and the doors opened. Gwen led the Aldens to a door at the end of the hallway. As she unlocked it, Henry looked out the hallway's window at the view of the city. The tops of the buildings made black and silver rectangles and triangles against the blue sky, and in some of the glass panels, he could see reflections of buildings nearby. To the east, they could see the banks of the Silver River. "Silver City looks amazing from up here!" Henry said.

"I wonder how many people are on just this block right now, in all these buildings," Benny said. "Probably a hundred."

"Oh, more than that," Henry said. "Probably thousands."

Secret on the Thirteenth Floor

"It *is* really strange that Gwen is having trouble renting out the apartments," Jessie said quietly, so Gwen wouldn't hear. "You would think people would be jumping at the chance to live in a building that has such a cool history and such great views."

"The history might be cool, but this place still gives me the creeps," said Benny. "If I was looking for a new apartment, I would keep looking."

Just then, Gwen swung open the apartment door. "Well," she said, "this will be your home for the next few days. Last year, this apartment was sitting empty, so I decided to stop trying to rent it out and instead fix it up as a guest suite for visitors. I hope you like it."

The girls stepped inside first, followed by Henry and Benny, and then Grandfather, who carried in the bags.

"Wow!" Violet said. The apartment's living room was full of antique furniture and rugs. An old crystal chandelier, which looked like it belonged in a ballroom, hung from the ceiling over a sloping velvet sofa with gold ribbon edging. On the walls were framed advertisements from the 1920s. One was for a train station. Another showed a woman in a beautiful gown, spraying a crystal bottle of perfume. "I feel like I'm in a movie," Violet said.

"Or a museum," Grandfather said with a laugh.

"The Bixby Museum," Gwen said, smiling. "I didn't have to go out and buy a single piece of furniture or decoration for it. You wouldn't believe the things people have left behind over the years, and I've kept them all. I know this probably sounds like something older people say all the time, but they really don't make things like they used to."

Benny glanced around the living room, looking a little confused. "But where is the TV?"

Jessie laughed. "Benny, TVs weren't common when most of this furniture and artwork was made."

Benny's eyes went wide. "Really?"

"People listened to the radio," Grandfather said. "They played cards and had dinner parties with music and dancing and conversation. I don't think they missed TV at all."

Gwen put her hand over her heart and said dreamily, "Don't you just wish you could go back in time?"

Secret on the Thirteenth Floor

She showed the children where to put their things in the bedroom and opened the antique refrigerator in the kitchen to show them that it only *looked* old on the outside. Inside, it looked like new, and the shelves were lined with cans of cream soda and lemonade, cups of yogurts, and a bowl of strawberries. "I put some snacks in here for you. Please help yourself," Gwen said.

"Maybe in a while," Henry said. "Right now, we'd love to know how we can get to work helping you with the building repairs."

Benny's face fell. He'd had his eye on the strawberries. But he knew Henry was right: work first, and then it would be time for snacks.

Gwen sighed. "Ah, yes," she said, "the repairs. Back to reality."

In the hallway, the Aldens waited once more for the elevator, but this time they only had to go up one floor. When the doors opened and they got inside, Benny went to press the button but then got confused. There was a button for each floor, including twelve, where they were now, but there was no button for the thirteenth floor. Even more confusing—at the top, there was a button for the *fourteenth* floor. He hadn't noticed it the last time they were in the elevator.

"Grandfather," Benny said, "didn't you tell us that the Bixby is thirteen stories tall?" Benny didn't like the idea that there might be hidden parts of the building.

"Oh, Benny, I apologize," Gwen said. She pressed the button for fourteen. "I forgot to explain another funny thing about this building. Remember how I told you people are superstitious about the thirteenth floor? Well, the most superstitious person in the Bixby is Felix, our superintendent. He takes care of all the building maintenance and fixes things that break—which, around here, happens all the time. He thinks it's bad luck to reference the number thirteen, so he changed the button for it to the fourteenth floor."

"That's funny," Jessie said. "It still says thirteen on the dial outside the elevator. But even if Felix changed that too, the floor is still in the same place. If thirteen *is* unlucky, wouldn't it still be unlucky even when Felix calls it something else?"

Gwen laughed. "That is a very sensible point, Jessie," she said.

"Anyway," Jessie said, "I don't believe there's anything unlucky about it, whatever you call it. Good luck and bad luck can happen anyplace."

Just then, the elevator jolted to a stop. Jessie stumbled forward and bumped into Henry. Henry bumped into Benny, who grabbed the bar on the elevator wall to stay on his feet.

"Whoa!" Grandfather said, putting his hands on Benny's shoulders to steady him.

"What's happening?" Violet asked in a small voice.

Gwen's eyes went wide. "I think the elevator is stuck."

"So good or bad luck can happen anyplace," Benny said. "But right now, it's happening on the thirteenth floor!"

Clue in the Ashes

Gwen pressed the red emergency button at the bottom of the panel. An alarm bell began to ring. "Don't worry," she told the Aldens. "This happens from time to time. It will just be a minute."

Sure enough, they soon heard a man's voice calling from outside the doors. "Hang on!" he said, and the doors opened just a crack. At the top, they saw two hands pulling the doors open, then a head and a pair of knees kneeling on the floor, which, strangely, was just above Grandfather's head.

"That's Felix," Gwen said to the Aldens.

"You're stuck between floors," the man said in a gruff voice. "I'm going to move the elevator manually. It'll just be a minute."

The doors closed again. "Well, this is an adventure!" Grandfather said.

A moment later, the elevator began to move up very slowly. When it stopped, the doors opened, and the floor was in the right place. Felix, a man with a long gray beard and denim overalls, was standing outside. Everyone got out to join him in the hallway. "That's a relief," Jessie said, putting her hand to her forehead.

"It nearly took longer to get to the thirteenth floor than it did to get to Silver City!" Grandfather said with a laugh.

Gwen looked at him with wide eyes and shook her head, but it was too late—Felix had already heard Grandfather mention the number thirteen.

"Please, sir, do not say that number aloud!" Felix said. "Here at the Bixby, it's 'fourteen' and 'fourteen' only." Felix pulled a silver chain from under the collar of his shirt. Hanging on it was something gray and furry. He closed his eyes and rubbed it between his fingers.

"Felix, what's that?" Violet asked.

"Young lady, that is my rabbit's foot," Felix said.

"A lot of people believe these can bring good luck, and we could use some around here. But you can't just count on the rabbit's foot. You have to stay away from all the things that bring bad luck."

Felix began to list some other things they should avoid. "Never break a mirror," Felix said, "or you'll have seven whole years of bad luck. Never let a black cat cross your path. Never walk under a ladder. And whatever you do, don't say the number thir—well, you know!"

"But why?" Jessie asked. "Why do people think those things are unlucky? And if they do have bad luck, how can they know the broken mirror or the black cat is the thing that's causing it, and not something else?"

"I really don't know the answer to those questions," Felix said. "All I know is that it's my duty to keep bad luck away from the Bixby. We get enough of it as it is."

"Felix is in the business of keeping us safe," Gwen said gently. "And we appreciate it."

Violet gave Jessie a confused look, and Jessie knew just what she was thinking: Did Gwen really believe in bad luck, or did she agree with Grandfather that it was just a coincidence when bad things happened? Why was Felix so upset? What did Gwen and Felix know that Grandfather didn't? The children would have to wait until they were alone to talk things over.

Grandfather told everyone he was going to lie down for a bit in the guest suite. "The drive tired me out," he said. "Plus, I have just two chapters left in my Patricia Dancy mystery novel, and I can't wait to find out who stole the diamonds on the train!" Grandfather started to get back into the elevator, but then he thought better of it. "You know, I think I have tested my luck enough for one day. I'll take the stairs."

"We'll see you at dinner, James," Gwen said to Grandfather with a smile as he waved and walked off. The girls thought this was a good sign because Gwen didn't seem nervous at all.

But Felix barely noticed that Grandfather had gone. He was still upset. "I'm telling you, Gwen, this problem with the elevator is another bad sign," Felix said, wringing his hands. "This floor is cursed!"

Gwen patted Felix's shoulder. "Well, I think we have a good sign too: these children have come to help us with the cleanup. What are the workers doing today?"

"Let's go have a look," Felix said. Gwen and the Aldens followed him past the closed doors of a few units that looked untouched. But at the end of the hallway was a door covered in black soot. The wallpaper surrounding it was also damaged with burn marks.

"I know it looks pretty bad," Gwen said. "But we've actually made a lot of progress inside the unit. Replacing this door will be the last part of the job."

Inside the apartment, a worker was installing new white cabinets in the kitchen, which was open to the living room. Two other men were hanging a light fixture, and another carefully carried a giant framed mirror across the living room and into one of the bedrooms.

Violet noticed that the walls were painted white, and the countertops in the kitchen were modern white stone. "The style of this apartment is different from the rest of the building," she said carefully. Violet didn't want to sound like she was criticizing Gwen's design choices, but she liked the antique look in the guest suite better.

Gwen sighed. "I know. These are the kinds of kitchens people seem to want these days—everything white and shiny. Since the old kitchen was destroyed in the fire, we thought we might as well upgrade."

The kitchen island was unfinished and still open on the bottom half. Standing in the living room, the children could see through it to the kitchen floor. Benny couldn't resist exploring such an inviting hiding place. He crawled inside.

"Benny, that's probably not a good idea," said Henry, reaching for his arm.

"Oh dear," Gwen said. "There are a lot of tools in here. Please be careful, Benny."

Benny crawled out on the kitchen side of the island. He noticed something metal in the corner, behind a trash bag.

"Hey, what's this?" Benny said as he picked up the object. It was made of aluminum that had once

been shiny but now was covered in black marks. On one end was a pointed nozzle. On the other end was a black handle and a plunger you could slide into the cylinder in the center. "It sort of looks like a water gun," Benny said.

He showed it to Henry. "I think it's some kind of tool," Henry said. "Maybe a caulking gun. You use those to seal the edges of windows and bathtubs and things like that."

Henry asked the worker in the kitchen if the tool belonged to him.

The man shook his head. "We found that on the floor. I was going to throw it away—looks like it got burned up pretty bad."

"You found it?" Felix asked.

"That's right," the worker said. He took a bandanna from his pocket and cleaned off his glasses. "We find all kinds of crazy things on job sites."

"I'm sure that's true," Felix said. "But there shouldn't have been anything to find in here. This unit was empty before the fire."

Gwen looked perplexed. "That is odd, Felix," she said. "But I guess it's possible we just missed something."

Just then, a man with curly black hair entered the apartment with a stack of cookie tins in his arms. He made his way around the living room, handing the tins out to the workers. Soon, all the power tools had gone silent, and the workers were taking a break, smiling and laughing and munching on cookies.

The scene made Gwen giggle. "It's like I always tell you, Hayes," Gwen said to the man when he joined the Aldens in the kitchen, "people get happier every time you enter a room."

"I think people just like cookies," Hayes said with a laugh. He had a booming voice and broad shoulders. Jessie thought he looked more like a weight lifter than a baker.

Hayes offered his hand and introduced himself to the children. "Would you like some cookies?" He opened the lid on a tin. Inside were three kinds: oatmeal raisin, chocolate peppermint, and coconut cream.

"I thought you'd never ask!" Benny said, and everyone laughed. Even Felix took a break from his worrying to enjoy the treats.

"Kids," Felix said, "Hayes lives on the twelfth floor. And we have him to thank for saving this building."

Hayes smiled shyly. "Oh, Felix, you're making too much of it."

"No, he's right," Gwen said. "If anything, I haven't thanked you enough." She turned to the Aldens. "Hayes smelled the smoke on the night of the fire, and that's how the firefighters were able to get here in time to put it out before it destroyed the rest of the building."

"My apartment is directly below this one," Hayes explained. "I was still awake when the fire started. As soon as I smelled it, I came up here to check it out. Then I called 911, which I'm sure you know is what you should do if you ever see a fire."

The children nodded. Felix told Gwen he wanted to show her the paint he had bought for one of the bedrooms, to make sure it was the right color. They left the kitchen, and Hayes remained with the children.

"I'm so glad you could come to help Gwen with the cleanup," Hayes said. "She works very hard to take care of this old building, and it's just a shame to see what has happened."

"We're happy to be here," Violet said. "We've never seen anyplace like the Bixby."

Hayes scratched his whiskers. "While you were

cleaning, did you happen to find anything... unusual?"

"Well," Henry said, "we just arrived and haven't done much work yet. But there is one thing."

Henry looked at Benny. "Yeah," Benny said, "just a minute ago, I found this on the floor. We were trying to figure out what it is. I thought maybe a squirt gun."

Hayes's eyes went wide when he saw the tool. "How strange," he said. "I'd be glad to take care of that for you. It looks damaged."

Benny pulled back his hand. "But I want to keep it." Benny had a growing squirt-gun collection at home, and he was thinking this would make a great addition. By July, when it was really hot, the Aldens would be all set to host a squirt-gun party in the backyard.

"Well," Jessie said, looking at the black soot smeared on Benny's palms from touching the tool, "let's at least leave it in here. It's too dirty to take back to the guest suite." Benny agreed. He put the squirt gun inside the cupboard beneath the sink and wiped his hands on a rag.

"Hayes, these cookies are awesome!" Benny said. "The coconut cream are my favorite."

"That's my grandmother's recipe," Hayes said. "She made them every Christmas. Well, it was lovely to meet you all, and thanks again for your help. I'm sure I'll be seeing you around this weekend."

The children said good-bye and headed back to the guest suite to get washed up for dinner. Grandfather was setting the large dining table and whistling. He seemed to be in a better mood than he had been on the thirteenth floor when the elevator got stuck.

Benny thought some of what had happened up there reminded him of watching a scary movie, but now that he was back in the guest suite, he was starting to relax a little. Nothing helped him get over being scared like the promise of food!

"What's for dinner?" Benny asked Grandfather.

"You're going to like this," Grandfather said. "Thai food! I got a few different noodle dishes, plus some chicken and rice and spring rolls. I ordered it a while ago, so it should be arriving any minute."

Benny licked his lips. There was still hope for

this day yet, despite its spooky beginning.

"How was your nap, Grandfather?" Violet asked. "Did you finish your book?"

"Yes, I did, and would you believe that the rich heiress turned out to be the one who stole the diamonds? No one suspected her. She was so wealthy they didn't think she had a motive. But the diamonds belonged to the man who had swindled her father years ago—it turns out she wanted revenge!"

Jessie smiled. "There's nothing like a good book," she said.

"And now I get to start another one, though I wish this author would write a little faster," Grandfather said. "I've nearly read them all. Maybe I will just have to settle for an interesting plot in real life when I see what jury duty is like."

The children laughed, then started getting ready for supper.

"I'll get us some cups," Henry said.

But Grandfather stopped him. "Actually, Henry, Gwen said we should use the crystal in the china cabinet for our drinks."

"Really?" Violet asked. "But it's so fragile."

"That's what I thought, but Gwen told me we shouldn't worry," Grandfather said. "These things were made to be used, not just looked at."

"This is going to be quite the fancy takeout dinner," Henry said.

"Cardboard and crystal," Grandfather said with a wink. "Only the best for the Aldens."

A Crash and a Creature

Late that night while the Aldens slept, the only sound in the guest suite was the ticking of an old grandfather clock that stood beside the fireplace. In one bedroom, Grandfather snored with his glasses still on and his new book open across his chest. In the other bedroom were the four children. Henry and Jessie slept in the matching twin beds under antique quilts. On the floor, Violet and Benny slept in sleeping bags.

Suddenly, a huge crash thundered through the apartment. Henry bolted up in bed. "What was *that*?" he said.

Violet rubbed her eyes and unzipped her bag. "I don't know. It sounded like it came from upstairs."

Benny and Jessie woke up too. "Do you think we should make sure everyone upstairs is okay?" Jessie asked.

Henry nodded. "Someone might need help."

The Aldens crept out of the bedroom in their pajamas and slippers. Violet peeked in on Grandfather. "He's still sound asleep," she said. "Let's not wake him."

Her sister and brothers agreed. They slipped into the hallway, which was dimly lit by brass light fixtures shaped like tulips, and walked single file to the elevator.

"Look," Jessie said, pointing to the half-moon dial. The hand was pointed to the number thirteen. "I think that means someone is upstairs."

"Let's go check it out," Benny said. He was about to press the *up* button when Henry put his hand on Benny's arm to stop him.

"Hang on," Henry said. "Are we sure the elevator is a good idea?"

"Good thinking," Jessie said. "It could get stuck again, and then what would we do? Let's take the stairs."

A Crash and a Creature

Henry held open the heavy door at the end of the hallway for the children to pass through, and then he eased it shut and followed them up the flight of stairs to the thirteenth—or fourteenth, depending on whom they asked—floor.

Except for a few tools piled outside the damaged unit, the thirteenth floor's hallway was the same as the hallway below—same red carpeting, same brass tulip light fixtures on the walls. But something about this floor in particular gave Benny a shiver. It was so dark and quiet, it reminded him of a haunted house he had once visited at a Halloween carnival. But that house had been quiet only until something creepy jumped out of a doorway.

Benny took a deep breath and tried to remind himself that the Bixby wasn't a haunted house, but he still wasn't completely sure as he followed his siblings to the damaged unit. Just before they reached it, something did jump out—a black shape—but it didn't make any noise, and it disappeared into a shadow.

Benny grabbed Jessie's hand. "Did you see that?"

Jessie nodded. Her eyes were wide. "It moved so

fast. It has to be some kind of animal."

"This is creepy!" Benny said in a loud whisper.

They waited to see if the shape would reappear. After a moment, two yellow eyes came into view, then two pointy ears, and a tail swishing back and forth. Jessie relaxed. "Oh, it's just a kitty!" she said.

The children got down on their knees and tried to call the cat over to them. It had a pretty face and a pink nose. "Meow," it said once, sounding friendly but shy. Then, suddenly startled by something, the cat raced off to the other end of the hallway.

Henry glanced behind them and was surprised to see Mrs. Mason standing in a fluffy blue bathrobe.

"What are you children doing up here?" she said. "It's the middle of the night."

"Hello, Mrs. Mason," said Henry, standing up and smoothing his pajama pants. "A loud crash woke us up, and we came to make sure everything was okay."

"It woke me up too," Mrs. Mason grumbled, leaning on her cane. "I can't get any peace and quiet around here."

Without explanation, Mrs. Mason walked toward the door of the apartment damaged in the fire. She opened it, and her cane clicked on the hardwood floor as she entered the apartment. The children followed her. Inside, she walked right past the kitchen and living room and headed for the bedroom. The Aldens had never been in this room before.

Mrs. Mason switched on the light. There on the floor was a pile of broken glass. Around the glass was a frame, with a few shards sticking from its corners.

"Well, there you have it," Mrs. Mason said. "The source of the big crash."

"Oh no," Jessie said. "We just saw the workers carrying this mirror in yesterday. It was brand-new."

"It may have been new, but it sure was ugly," Mrs. Mason said.

Henry scratched his head. "That is really strange. How could a new mirror just break on its own like that? No one was in here."

"It's possible it was damaged when they moved it or when they hung it up," Jessie said. "Maybe it had a little crack and it finally gave out?"

"Or maybe someone *was* in here, and they left after it broke," Violet said.

"Oh, don't be ridiculous," Mrs. Mason said. "Who would be up here in the middle of the night?"

"I don't like this," Benny said. "Remember what Felix said? It's bad luck to break a mirror—*seven years* of bad luck! Does the bad luck affect just the person who breaks the mirror, or everyone nearby? Seven years means I would be"—Benny stopped to count on his fingers—"thirteen when the bad luck finally wore off!"

"Oh, Benny, that's just a superstition, remember?" Jessie said, patting Benny's shoulder to reassure him. "Felix is a nice man, and he's working very hard to take care of the building, but there are other explanations for these things. We don't have to worry about bad luck."

Benny wasn't so sure.

"I think we all need to get some sleep," Mrs. Mason said.

"Yes," Henry said. "You're right. Good night, Mrs. Mason."

She only harrumphed and walked back into

the hallway. The children turned off the light and closed the door to the apartment. On the way back to the stairs, Violet said, "I wonder what happened to that cat. She looked really afraid."

Benny stopped, his eyes suddenly wide. "Wait. Remember when Felix said, 'Never break a mirror'?"

Jessie sighed. "Really, Benny, we've been over this. Everything's okay."

Benny shook his head. "He also said, 'Don't let a black cat cross your path.' We never saw that cat anywhere in this building—except the thirteenth floor. What if this is part of the curse? I'm going to have bad luck until I'm twenty!"

Violet looked at Henry and Jessie with worry in her eyes. "It is a strange coincidence," she said. "And it *was* completely black—it didn't even have a spot of gray or brown."

"That was just a sweet cat, not a bad sign," Henry said. "In the morning, we can ask Gwen about it. It probably belongs to one of the tenants. You'll see."

The children crept back into the apartment and were relieved to see that all the noise had not woken Grandfather. They got back into their beds and sleeping bags, and soon Henry could hear Benny's and Violet's breathing change. He knew they were asleep.

"Jessie? Are you still awake?" Henry whispered.

Jessie turned onto her side and propped her head up on her elbow. "Yeah."

"I'm not scared of that cat, are you?"

"No," Jessie said. "You're right. There's no such thing as a curse."

"But I *am* worried about something else," Henry said. "Upstairs, Mrs. Mason seemed to appear out of nowhere. And she took us right to where the broken mirror was, almost like she already knew what had made the noise. How did she get upstairs so fast?"

Jessie thought about this for a moment. "That's a very good question," she said.

***

The next morning was Sunday, and the Aldens were up and dressed before Grandfather was awake. He was enjoying his last morning of sleeping in before his jury duty would begin Monday morning.

Secret on the Thirteenth Floor

"I want one more look at that mirror," Benny said. "I almost wonder if it was all a bad dream."

This time the children took the elevator to the thirteenth floor, and it worked just fine. When the doors opened, they realized they weren't the only ones curious about what had happened the night before. As they walked down the hallway, they heard voices coming from the damaged apartment.

"Listen, Gwen," Felix was saying as the Aldens entered the bedroom to find him, along with Gwen, Hayes, and Mrs. Mason. "I know you've been skeptical of my thoughts on this, but you can't get a worse sign than a broken mirror! Especially since there wasn't a soul around—it really looks like this mirror broke out of the blue. Now, how do you explain that?"

Gwen had her arms crossed and looked like she was struggling to be patient as she listened to the others' opinions. While Felix worriedly kneaded the back of his neck and rubbed his rabbit's foot between his fingers, Mrs. Mason poked the pile of broken glass with her cane. "Maybe the Bixby doesn't like these new decorations you keep trying to put up on her walls. This beautiful old building is fighting back. That's what I think!" Mrs. Mason said.

"I wouldn't blame the Bixby for rejecting some of these changes, but let's be reasonable," Hayes said. "Did anyone see anything strange last night?"

"No one could have been in here. The door was locked last night," Felix said. "I'm sure of it. I've been extra careful since the fire."

The Aldens shared a glance. They *had* seen something strange, but they kept the details about the black cat to themselves. They wanted to be able to ask Gwen about it in private first.

Gwen cleared her throat. "Thank you for your interest in figuring out what happened, but right now, my main concern is to get this room cleaned up before someone gets hurt on the glass." She gestured toward the children. "And I see that my helpers have arrived just in time, thank goodness. Why don't the rest of you get on with your day? I promise to let you know as soon as I learn anything about how the mirror got broken."

After Hayes, Mrs. Mason, and Felix had left the

apartment, Gwen found a broom and dustpan and handed them to Henry.

"Henry, I'll take that," Benny said, sweeping up the glass. "Maybe if I help clean up the broken mirror, I can get some of my luck back."

"Benny, I don't think you have to worry about your luck, but I do appreciate all the help you kids have been," Gwen said.

"We're happy to do it," Jessie said.

Gwen held open a trash bag so Benny could pour the glass into it from the dustpan. "If I can't get to the bottom of the problems on this floor, I'm worried people will start moving out. The new high-rise building next door—the one with a pool on the roof—is running a special to attract new tenants: half off your first month's rent *and* free cable. I just can't compete with that," Gwen said.

"Don't worry, Gwen," said Violet. "We're going to help you figure out what's going on."

Henry looked at Jessie, and she nodded, encouraging him to bring up what they'd seen the night before. "We wanted to ask you about something," Henry said. "Last night, when we heard the crash, we came up here to make sure everything was okay. In the hallway, we saw a black cat. Does it belong to someone who lives here?"

Gwen looked puzzled. "A cat? I don't think so. When I bought the building, I decided to make it pet-free so the new carpet would stay nice longer. I would be quite alarmed if there were any pets in my building."

Gwen told the children she needed to get back to her office to take care of some bills. When she was gone, Jessie turned to Henry. "Okay, even though I don't believe in bad luck, I have to admit that the cat is pretty spooky. No animals at all in the building? Where did that cat come from?"

"I don't know," Henry said. "But there has to be an explanation. Cats don't just appear out of nowhere, and they don't bring bad luck."

"Henry, there are just too many weird things going on up here," Benny said. "What could explain them all?" Suddenly he got a funny look on his face and went quickly out of the bedroom and down the hall. Henry and the girls heard cupboard doors opening and closing in the kitchen. Then Benny ran back into the bedroom.

"And here's another weird thing: my squirt gun!" Benny said. "The one we found yesterday. It's gone!"

CHAPTER 5

In the Dark

On Monday, the Alden children continued their work on the apartment while Gwen drove Grandfather to the courthouse, where he was supposed to report for jury duty. Gwen offered to bring them along and give them a tour of some of the other buildings downtown, but Henry said they'd like to get some work done first. Of course, the Aldens were glad to help out, but they also knew spending time in the apartment might give them a better chance of solving the mystery.

In her notebook, Jessie made a list of the work left to do to get the apartment ready for a new tenant.

1. Hang pictures in front bedroom
2. Paint last wall in back bedroom

3. Carry old bathroom tile to garbage

4. Wash bathroom floor

Henry found a pair of gloves and began stacking up the squares of cracked and stained ceramic tile that the workers had removed before putting in the new bathroom floor. Violet used a flat-head screwdriver to open a can of robin's-egg-blue paint, and she and Benny got to work finishing painting in the back bedroom. In the kitchen, Jessie poured soap into a bucket and put it under the faucet to fill. Then she found a paint-speckled radio under the sink, plugged it in, and turned to a station playing Motown music.

The children couldn't help but dance a little bit while they worked. The songs made the time pass more quickly—and they made Benny forget about the strange things that were happening on the thirteenth floor.

Soon a few workers arrived to finish up the kitchen cabinets and install a new air conditioner. Henry carried a crate of old tile down to the garbage.

In the bedroom, Benny climbed the ladder with his paintbrush to finish off the top corner of the wall. When they had started the job, the morning sun had been shining into the room and providing plenty of light. But now the sky was cloudy, and the room had grown dim.

"Violet, could you turn on the light?" Benny asked.

"Sure," Violet said. She set down her brush and flicked the switch. The bulb flared for a second, but then they heard a loud *pop* and the lights went out. The Motown music went silent.

"What was that?" Benny asked, looking around, worried.

Violet looked up at Benny. "Don't move," she said. "I'm coming to help you down."

"Okay, but don't walk under the ladder!" Benny said.

Violet stopped. "Why not?"

"Remember what Felix said? It's bad luck to walk under a ladder."

"I think that's probably a superstition, Benny," Violet said. But she decided to go around the ladder, just to be on the safe side. She reached out her hand and helped Benny step down to the floor. "Don't worry."

Violet and Benny joined Jessie in the living room.

"What do you think happened?" Jessie asked one of the workers. He set down his drill and wiped his hands on a rag from his pocket.

"Felix told us this floor is cursed," Benny said. "Do you think so too?"

In the Dark

"Well, let's take a look," the worker said. The children joined him in the kitchen, where he removed the plate covering the electrical outlet and peered inside the wall with his flashlight. He whistled long and low. "Now *that* is some old-fashioned wiring," he said.

The other worker joined him and laughed when he saw the crusty-looking cords poking out of the wall. "You might even call it *antique*, though it's not the kind of antique anyone would want in their house."

The first worker turned to Benny. "Take a look in there, little fella," he said, and he held the flashlight so Benny could see. "The electricity went out because of bad wiring. Superstitions— worries about bad luck and curses—those are just explanations for things that people can't understand or see. In this case, we can say for sure that a mechanical problem is to blame."

Henry came back into the apartment. "It smells like something's burning in here," he said. Jessie explained what had happened, and the worker with the flashlight told him the bad wiring could be a fire hazard. "This will need to be fixed by an electrician right away," he said.

"What's that I hear?" Gwen asked. She had just returned from delivering Grandfather to the courthouse. "Another bill to pay?"

"I'm afraid so," the worker said to Gwen. "You don't want to take any chances with electrical work."

"Gwen," said Henry, "do you think this could have caused the fire?"

Gwen thought that over. "I guess it's possible," she said. "But that would mean someone had to have been in this apartment and turned on the light. As far as I know, it was empty when the fire started. And no one has come forward to tell me otherwise."

"What about the elevator?" Jessie asked. "Could the old wiring have caused that to stop?"

Gwen shrugged. "I really don't know. What do you think, guys?" she asked the workers.

Both men shook their heads. "No, I don't think so," said the man who had uncovered the outlet. "If the elevator stopped, that was done by someone on purpose."

In the Dark

"Or *something*," said Benny. "Maybe the building did it on its own."

"Oh, Benny," said Jessie. "That's nonsense. We just need more information to figure out how it happened."

"Gwen," said Henry, "do you think we could go down to the basement and take a look at the elevator's controls? Maybe we'll find something to explain what happened."

Gwen shrugged. "I don't see why not," she said. "Let's check it out."

Henry asked the worker if he could borrow his flashlight, and together, the Aldens and Gwen took the elevator to B for basement. The doors opened to reveal a very old-looking room. Bare bulbs hung from the rafters, making a yellow glow on the worn concrete floor. A pile of old furniture stood in the corner beside some abandoned bikes. Along the back wall stood a row of huge iron tanks with pipes leading up to the ceiling.

"What are those?" Benny asked, pointing at them, his eyes wide.

"Those are the boilers that make all the hot

water for the building," Gwen explained. "We've had them updated a little, but they are still the original tanks, made out of solid cast iron. They hold a lot of water and still work pretty great. And thank goodness. I can't imagine how much they weigh—or how we would ever get them out of here if they broke!"

She led the children around to the back of the elevator shaft to a small control room. Gwen used her key to open the door, and the Aldens followed her inside, though the room was so small they could barely fit. Henry turned on the flashlight and shined it at the wall. A rectangular panel was mounted there, and lights on the panel showed what floor the elevator was on. A glass casing with a black handle protected the elevator panel. Jessie took a step forward. As she looked more closely, she gasped. "The handle is broken!"

"It is?" Gwen asked. Jessie showed her how the handle had been yanked out of place. It hung down at a strange angle. "Yikes. This is not good," Gwen said.

"Who would have done this?" Violet asked.

"Well, another question might be who *could*

have done this," Gwen said. "There's only one other person besides me who has a key to this control room: Felix!"

Saucy Sal's

Late that afternoon, the children returned to the guest suite to get cleaned up. Violet's and Benny's hands were spotted with blue paint, and Jessie had some construction dust in her hair. After they had gotten showered and dressed, Grandfather came home.

"How did it go?" Jessie asked.

"Well, it was a little dull," Grandfather said with a smile. "Like many important things in life, jury duty involves a lot of waiting around. We spent a couple hours hearing testimony this morning, but then the judge called a recess, and the lawyers settled the case. So the judge dismissed us."

"So you spent most of your day in a waiting

room?" Jessie asked. She thought that sounded awfully boring.

"Yes, but I had Patricia Dancy's next mystery novel with me. I finished the whole thing!"

"Wow!" Jessie said.

"What about the pizza?" Benny asked. "Did it have pepperoni?"

Grandfather laughed. "No pizza this time, Benny. I only had an egg sandwich out of a vending machine. I guess only juries on cases that last a whole day get pizza."

"Well, it's almost dinnertime," Benny said with a gleam in his eye. "Maybe there's still time for this to turn into a pizza day!"

"Hope springs eternal," Grandfather said. He thought for a minute and then clapped his hands when an idea came to him. "And I have just the place!"

***

Saucy Sal's was in a small brick building in a somewhat deserted neighborhood on the west side of Silver City. From the outside, the children noticed the restaurant looked a little run-down. The C in the red neon sign over the door was burned out, and the paint on the green shutters was peeling.

"Are you sure this is the right place?" Benny asked.

Grandfather nodded as he pulled the car into a parking space. "Oh yes," he said. "Saucy Sal's is famous for serving the best Silver City-style pizza."

"What makes it Silver City style?" Henry asked.

"You'll see," Grandfather said as they went in. The inside of the restaurant couldn't have been more different from its outside. A crowd of people stood in front of a counter, and behind it was a teenage girl wearing a red shirt and a name tag that said SUE. With a big smile for each person who came in, she wrote down the names of the groups and handed out menus for the customers to read over while they waited. In the main dining room, cheerful red booths lined one wall, and all the tables were covered with brown paper. Some children nearby were drawing a treasure map on their table with crayons. A balloon was tied to each child's chair.

"This is such a happy place!" Violet said.

Saucy Sal's

"Does everyone get a balloon?" Benny asked.

Grandfather nodded. "That's the way they've done things at Saucy Sal's for decades. Their old commercial used to say, 'If you leave sad, your meal is free!'"

It was difficult for the children to wait for their turn to be seated. The restaurant was full of the delicious smell of bread and cheese and garlic, and they could almost taste the pizza. Just when their patience was about to wear out, Sue called, "Alden, party of five?"

Benny leaped from his chair. "That's us!"

Benny led his siblings and grandfather as they followed the waitress on a winding path through the main dining room and around a corner to a quieter side room with a large, round table. The children took their places and ordered drinks—lemonade for Benny and Jessie, root beer for Violet, and water for Henry and Grandfather—and then Grandfather ordered a large Silver City-style pizza. The waitress gave each of the Aldens a balloon, and they helped each other tie the strings to their chairs.

Secret on the Thirteenth Floor

From where they were on the far side of the city, they could see the whole skyline out the window.

"I just love Silver City," Jessie said with a sigh, resting her cheek on her fist. "It's so exciting to think that people come here from all over to work and live. Silver City is the perfect name. Everything is so new and shiny!"

"Some of it is new," Violet said. "But some of it has been here for a long time. I think that the history of this place is what makes it so great. Think of all the different people who have come here from all over to start a new life. It's so inspiring!"

"And think of the different *foods* from all over the world!" Benny said.

"Benny," Grandfather said, "you show remarkable focus!"

"I really hope we can figure out what's happening at the Bixby building," Violet said, "and convince people not to be afraid of living there."

"Grandfather," Jessie said, "do you know why Felix has so many superstitions? It seems like he's afraid of so many funny things: ladders, broken mirrors, cats, numbers. Has he really seen bad things come from them?"

Grandfather thought about this. "I guess it's possible he has, but the most likely explanation is that those were coincidences. If he walked under a ladder and then lost his wallet, he might think walking under the ladder caused him to lose his wallet. But really it was just two things happening on the same day."

"But why is he worried about mirrors but not other things made of glass, like windows?" Jessie asked.

"Many superstitions are based on beliefs people had a long time ago, before we had modern science to help us understand the world," Grandfather explained. "For instance, the fear of ladders goes back to ancient Egypt, I believe. Ladders make the shape of a triangle, which was considered sacred, and Egyptians believed that walking through it was disrespectful. Disrespect could make the gods angry, and then bad things would happen to you as a result."

Henry's eyebrows went up. "Maybe Felix is interested in ancient Egypt."

"Maybe," Grandfather said. "Or maybe he doesn't even know about that history. That's the funny thing about superstitions. People who believe in them often don't know why they do. Knowing the story behind them actually can make people feel less afraid."

"What do you think, Benny?" Jessie asked. "Does knowing the story help?"

"A little," Benny said. "But the thirteenth floor is still spooky."

Just then, the waitress arrived at the table with a giant tray. Silver City-style pizza turned out to be constructed of thin layers of crust and cheese, stacked one on top of the other, a little like lasagna. On the very top was a thick layer of sauce and another layer of cheese. Grandfather used a large knife to cut the pizza and scoop it onto the children's plates. In the sauce were the toppings that would usually be on top of a pizza: sausage, pepperoni, mushrooms.

Henry was the first to take a bite. "Yum!" he said.

"Mmm, I love all the cheese," Violet said.

"And the sauce! It's spicy!" added Jessie.

"Mmfffghhh," said Benny. His mouth was full, and even though the children couldn't understand what he was saying, they agreed. Everyone loved Silver City-style pizza!

Grandfather cut everyone a second piece and

then excused himself to go say hello to the owner of the restaurant, whom he'd been friends with for many years. While he was gone, the children went over what they had learned about the mysterious events in the Bixby.

"I keep thinking about that black cat," Violet said. "Where did it come from?"

"And I have a funny feeling about Mrs. Mason," Jessie said. "She isn't very kind."

"I hate to say it, but I agree," said Violet.

"She isn't very kind," Henry said. "But that doesn't mean she would try to scare people."

"You're right," Jessie said, taking a sip of her lemonade, "but it's strange how she suddenly appeared when the mirror broke. And then she took us right into the bedroom of that apartment. She didn't seem at all surprised when we saw the broken glass—it was as if she already knew what happened before we got there."

Henry nodded. "I was thinking about that too. If she came up in the elevator, wouldn't we have heard the bell make a noise?"

"She could have taken the stairs," Violet suggested.

Benny said. "What about Hayes?"

Grandfather returned to the table but didn't interrupt the conversation.

"I think he seems really friendly," Violet said. "After all, look at all the cookies he baked for the workers."

"Yes," Henry said, "but remember how he asked whether we had found anything in the apartment yesterday? When he saw that water gun, or whatever it was, it seemed like he wanted to take it."

"Well," Violet said, "maybe he was just nervous about the rumors that the floor is cursed. We've all been pretty nervous about that!"

"Maybe no one is doing these things," Benny suggested. "Maybe the building really is cursed and trying to scare people away."

Jessie shook her head. "That's impossible, Benny. There has to be an explanation. Why didn't Hayes come up to the thirteenth floor when the mirror broke? Isn't his apartment below the apartment where they had the fire? It seems like he would have heard the crash—we heard it all the way at the end of the hall."

Secret on the Thirteenth Floor

"That's a good question, Jessie," Henry said. He wiped some sauce from his chin with a napkin. "It's possible Hayes wasn't home, but we'll have to find out. And then there's one more mysterious person at the Bixby—Felix."

"He has so many superstitions, and I can't tell if Gwen shares them," Jessie said.

"I don't think he's trying to scare people on purpose," Violet said. "But on the other hand, he's the only other person who has a key to the control room for the elevator."

"This conversation sounds just like jury duty," Grandfather said. "Everyone trying to figure out who did what."

The children turned to their Grandfather. "What was the case about?" Jessie asked.

"Well, I can only talk about it because it was dismissed by the judge," Grandfather said. "Otherwise, I'd have to keep it a secret. But it was a robbery. And the only reason the person got caught was that he returned to the scene of the crime. This happens in a lot of cases. Someone who made a bad choice and committed a crime just can't help going back to the place where it happened."

Jessie sat up straight and grabbed Henry's arm. "Does that remind you of anything?" she asked.

"What do you mean?" said Henry.

"It's like that squirt gun Benny found," Jessie said. "He put it in the cupboard, planning to come back for it later, but when he did, it was gone. Someone came back for it. Someone returned to the scene of the crime!"

Henry nodded. "I think you must be right, Jessie."

"But why was that thing so important that it would be worth coming back for?" Jessie asked.

The Big Spill

The next day, the Aldens woke up early to cook breakfast for Gwen, Felix, and the workers, who had been putting many hours into restoring the apartment damaged in the fire. Jessie and Violet made an egg-and-broccoli casserole, and Henry and Benny toasted a whole loaf of bread and arranged dishes of butter and jam on the long dining table in the guest suite. They set the places with pink china rimmed in gold, which they had found in the hutch.

"This smells wonderful!" Gwen said as she led the group to the table. "And I'm so happy to see this old china getting some use."

The workers and Felix echoed her good mood as

they took their places. Grandfather began passing the food around.

Jessie dried her hands on a towel. She and the other children had eaten breakfast when they first woke up, so they were ready to get to work. "Enjoy your food," Jessie said. "We'll see you in a little while."

"Don't work too hard!" Gwen called after them.

The Aldens took the elevator upstairs and walked down the hallway to the apartment. With the electricity out the day before, they hadn't been able to finish hanging pictures on the walls, and they hoped to get it done now. As they walked, Violet stopped every few feet and turned to look behind them.

"Violet, what are you doing?" Jessie asked.

"Looking for the cat," Violet said. "I know we didn't just imagine it. It has to be around here someplace."

Inside the apartment, a bad surprise was waiting. "Oh no!" Henry said when he saw the kitchen. The cabinets were finished and the island was complete, but the newly finished wood floor was now covered in two shades of blue paint, one light and one dark. Two cans lay on their sides in the middle of an enormous paint puddle.

"I don't think this is part of the new design," said Benny.

Violet's hands flew to her mouth. "This is terrible," she whispered.

"Do you think someone did this on purpose?" Henry asked.

"They must have," Jessie said, shaking her head. "The last time we were here, those cans were in the bedroom with their lids on tight."

"Or maybe the broken mirror and the black cat passed bad luck onto the person who spilled them!" Benny said.

The children ran down the hallway. They were in too much of a hurry to wait for the elevator, so they took the stairs instead and raced into the guest suite.

Gwen dropped her fork and stood up when she saw their faces. "What's wrong?"

"Something's happened in the apartment," Henry said. "Paint is spilled all over the kitchen

floor...and it looks like someone did it on purpose."

Felix threw down his napkin. "I was afraid of this," he said, and grabbed the rabbit's foot he wore on his chain. "After all, it *is* May thirt—well, it's the day after the twelfth. Oh, how I hate that number."

"Now, Felix," Gwen started.

Felix shook his head. "Bad signs always come in threes: first there was the fire, then the broken mirror, and now this."

Two women who lived on the tenth floor popped their heads into the guest suite, each of them holding a tennis racket. "Gwen, we've been looking for you," one woman said. "We just heard what's happened on the thirteenth floor. Everyone is talking about the bad luck. Today is our league championship match—what if we lose? Something has to be done about the thirteenth floor!"

Felix put his hands over his ears. "Ugh! Don't say that number."

The other tenant pointed her racket at Gwen. "If this doesn't stop soon, we are going to break our lease and move out!"

Everyone at the table began discussing their

The Big Spill

opinions on the strange events, and the talk soon broke into an argument. Gwen raised her voice above the others. "Please, everyone! Let's try to stay calm."

Grandfather sighed. "Yes, Gwen is right. We have to keep our heads."

"Felix," Jessie said, trying to keep her voice friendly, "I know it seems like all these things are related, but it really is just a coincidence that so many bad things have happened upstairs. The numbers are just numbers, whether you are talking about *three* or *thirteen*. Not only that, but when you said bad things happen in threes, you forgot to include the broken fireplace, the stuck elevator, and the electricity going out. So that actually makes six things. If you string enough superstitions together, you can make up a story for just about anything. But that doesn't mean it's true."

"Well said," said the worker who had helped the Aldens look inside the electrical outlet the day before. "There is a reasonable explanation. We just don't know what it is yet."

But Felix and the tenants from the tenth floor

did not look convinced. And poor Gwen looked more worried than ever. Behind her cheerful red glasses, her eyes began to fill with tears.

Grandfather crossed to her side of the table and patted her shoulder. "Don't worry, my friend. We are going to get to the bottom of this."

"And in the meantime," Violet said, "we are going to clean up that paint."

Gwen and the children returned to the apartment on the thirteenth floor and got to work with a stack of rags, mopping up as much of the paint as they could and then using buckets of hot, soapy water to wash up the rest. The floorboards would probably have to be sanded down and refinished to get rid of all the blue marks.

Violet gazed at the floor with her artist's eye. "If you can get over the damage, the streaks of blue are sort of pretty in a way."

Gwen laughed. "I love how you always see the possibilities in things, Violet. Maybe we should leave it as it is. We could start a new trend—paint-smeared flooring!"

Violet laughed. "Well," she said, "I prefer the

blue spots to all the black burn marks that must have been on the floor after the fire."

"You know," Gwen said as she squeezed blue water out of a sponge, "all the burn marks were actually on the ceiling. We just decided to use the opportunity to redo the floor while the apartment was empty."

"But how come the fire only damaged the ceiling?" Violet asked.

"Heat rises," Jessie said. "Smoke always goes up. So if this building had a fourteenth floor—a real fourteenth floor—people on that floor would have been the first to smell the smoke."

Henry thought about this. "That's right, Jessie. And that makes me wonder something: If the smoke was rising, damaging the ceiling and not the floor, why did Hayes smell smoke down on the twelfth floor?"

Benny opened his mouth to suggest an answer, but before he could get a word out, a loud siren began echoing through the Bixby's hallways.

"Oh no!" Gwen said. "That's the smoke alarm!"

8

Smoky Secret

Gwen and the children raced down the stairs and through the hallway on the twelfth floor, following the sound of the screeching smoke alarm. It led them to Hayes's apartment, and they found him in his kitchen, waving a towel in front of the open window. Black smoke poured from a muffin tin sitting on the stove top.

Hayes cringed when he saw the Aldens. "I'm so embarrassed!" he said. "I was baking these cupcakes for my friend's birthday. I doubled the recipe but then completely forgot about the second pan in the oven and went into my room to read. I guess I must have fallen asleep and"—Hayes threw up his hands in frustration—"well, you can see what happened."

He swished the towel above his head, where the smoke detector was mounted on the ceiling. After a moment, the loud screeching finally stopped.

"Don't worry, Hayes," Henry said. "Everyone makes mistakes."

"That's right," Benny said. He was about to share the story of the time he tried to make cookies but left out the eggs by accident. But then he noticed something surprising—and familiar. On the counter, next to a tray of cupcakes covered in frosting, lay the tool he had thought was a squirt gun when he'd found it in the damaged apartment. It had disappeared, and now here it was in Hayes's kitchen! It was a kitchen tool, for piping frosting onto cupcakes.

"Hayes," Benny said, "why didn't you tell me that frosting tool belonged to you when I found it? I would have given it back to you."

Hayes sighed. "Boy, nothing gets past you kids." He took a moment to hang the towel back on the rack. He seemed to be thinking. When he turned around, he said, "Gwen, I need to be honest with you about something."

Smoky Secret

"I always appreciate honesty," Gwen said encouragingly.

"You've given me so much credit for alerting everyone about the fire in time to save the building, and I guess I did do that, but I haven't told you the whole truth about how I discovered there was a fire. I didn't smell smoke and run upstairs to see what was happening. I was already on the thirteenth floor. I was in that apartment."

Gwen's eyebrows shot up. "You were? But why?"

Hayes sighed. "I was making a complicated layer cake that required the two parts of the cake to be baked at different temperatures. I needed a second oven. I knew no one was living up there, and I didn't think it would do any harm to borrow the oven for an hour."

"Oh, Hayes," Gwen said.

"I put one cake layer in on the thirteenth floor, and then I ran back downstairs to my apartment to put the second layer in my oven. When I went up to check on the first layer, I came upon the fire in the kitchen."

"So the fire started in the oven?" Henry asked.

Hayes shook his head. "I don't think so. When I went up to the apartment on thirteen, I turned on the light and the oven and put my cake in. There was a little burning smell, but I figured it was just old crumbs in the bottom of the oven, because it hadn't been cleaned in a long time. So I went back downstairs. But when I returned a few minutes later, there was a fire."

"I figured it was the wiring," Gwen said. "But by the time the firefighters got here, all the walls in the kitchen were black. It was hard to tell where the fire started and what path it took as it spread."

"I suppose you would have found out eventually," Hayes said, "when the firefighters filed their report."

"Probably so," Gwen said, "but either way, I'm glad you told me."

"I'm sorry I lied," Hayes said. "I have regretted it ever since. It feels terrible to keep a secret like that."

"It's okay," Gwen said. "It sounds like one bad choice that just got out of hand."

"Yes," Hayes said. "It was a bad choice. But I swear to you that I don't know anything about the other strange events up there since the fire. I know my word doesn't mean much anymore, but I hope you will believe me. I did not break the mirror or spill that paint."

"I believe you," Gwen said.

"So do I," said Jessie.

"And you're sure you can't remember anything else that might help us figure out who is responsible?" Henry asked.

Hayes pressed his lips together. "There is one thing," he said. "The night you first arrived, I snuck back into that apartment to get my piping tool. I was worried the apartment would be locked, but it wasn't. And not only that—someone else was inside! I heard them moving around in the bedroom, and then I heard the mirror break. I grabbed my tool and ran out of there."

"And how did you get back to the twelfth floor?" Benny asked.

"I didn't want to wait for the elevator and risk being seen, so I took the stairs," Hayes said.

"We must have just missed you," Benny said. "Because we took the stairs up to see what made the noise."

"Hayes, did you get a look at the person who was in the apartment?" Gwen asked.

"No," Hayes said. "But there was one thing: I heard a kind of clicking sound on the hardwood floor. Could that be a clue?"

The Aldens looked at one another. They had heard clicking on the hardwood floor that night too. "I think I know who we should talk to next," said Jessie.

9

A Blue Clue

When the Aldens knocked, it took a while for Mrs. Mason to answer the door. They heard the clicking of her cane as she approached.

"What is it?" she said, opening the door. Her reading glasses were pushed up on her hair, and she had a newspaper under her arm. "I guess there really is no such thing as peace and quiet around here."

"Mrs. Mason," Henry said, "we were wondering if you could help us figure out what might have happened the other night with the broken mirror."

Just then, Violet noticed something strange about Mrs. Mason's shoes: last time she had seen them, they were white, but now they had streaks of blue on the sides. Violet elbowed Benny and pointed at them.

Benny's eyes went wide. "You have blue paint on your shoes!"

Mrs. Mason stared at the children for a moment. Her face started to turn red, as if she was getting ready to yell. But suddenly her anger deflated like a balloon, and her shoulders fell. She tossed the newspaper on the table behind her and opened her apartment door wide. "Please. Come in," Mrs. Mason said.

The Aldens gave each other bewildered looks, but they followed Mrs. Mason inside and sat on the living room couch. Gwen sat in a nearby chair, and Mrs. Mason took a seat across from them.

"I suppose there's no reason to keep on pretending," Mrs. Mason said. "I broke the mirror and spilled the paint."

"You did?" Henry asked.

Mrs. Mason nodded. "And after I saw you in the lobby, I stopped the elevator to make it seem like it was broken."

"But how did you get into the control room?" Violet asked.

Secret on the Thirteenth Floor

Mrs. Mason reached into the pocket of her pants and pulled out something that jangled. "I have a set of keys. Sam, the man who owned the Bixby before Gwen, gave them to me. He and I were close friends."

The children turned to Gwen, who was sitting very still with her hands in her lap and a shocked look on her face. In a timid voice, she said, "But why, Mrs. Mason? Why would you do these things?"

"I heard Felix talking about his superstitions," Mrs. Mason said, "and I noticed that some people in the building believed his idea that there was a curse on the thirteenth floor. They were afraid. I guess I saw the chance to stoke their fears. I didn't want a new tenant to move into the apartment above me. Like I always say, I just want some peace and quiet."

"Why didn't you just tell me your feelings about the upstairs apartment?" Gwen said. "Maybe we could have worked something out."

"You're right," Mrs. Mason said. "I should have. I'm sorry for what I did—sorry for scaring anyone and sorry for the damage I've caused. I'd like to try to make it up to you."

"Well," Gwen said, "for starters, we could use some help fixing the access box in the elevator control room. It's still broken."

"I will pay for the repair," Mrs. Mason said, "and for the floor to be fixed. I just wish so much wasn't changing around here. The Bixby is a classic. Everything about this old place is perfect."

For the first time since the mystery was solved, Gwen smiled. "I love the Bixby too. You know I do. But this building is not perfect. No building is. If we want to make sure it's still standing for another generation to enjoy, we have to make updates. I do agree with you that we should be careful about what we change. We don't want to lose any of the things that make the Bixby so special."

"My thoughts exactly," Mrs. Mason said. Just then, a dark shape darted out from the hallway and leaped into Mrs. Mason's lap.

Violet's hand went to her mouth. "You have a black cat!"

"Well, now all my secrets are coming out," Mrs. Mason said, smiling.

Gwen looked at the cat in shock. "Mrs. Mason,"

Gwen said, "this is supposed to be a pet-free building!"

Mrs. Mason laughed. "I know. It's funny—back when Sam owned the building, I never wanted to have a cat, but when you made a rule against it, the first thing I did was go out and get one. I really didn't like the way you were changing so many things around here, but it wasn't very nice of me to lie."

"If I let you keep the cat," Gwen said, "I'm going to have to let other people have pets too."

"That wouldn't be so bad, would it?" Mrs. Mason asked. "I like seeing life in the hallways here. It takes me back to old times, when the Bixby was a happier place."

Gwen thought for a moment and nodded. "You're right, Mrs. Mason. Not all the changes I've made have been good ones. And as far as the building goes, maybe you could help me make a plan? We could take a walk around the halls and list the special pieces—artwork, lights, woodwork—that we want to save. And we'll make sure the workers understand they can't just rip things out. They have to work around the special pieces that give this building such great character."

Mrs. Mason scratched the cat's ears. "I'd be honored to help you," she said.

"What's the cat's name?" Violet asked.

"I call her Jinx!" Mrs. Mason said. They all laughed. A cat named Jinx was a perfect fit for the Bixby.

The Aldens decided to let the women talk out the plans on their own. It was time to get back to the guest suite and pack up their suitcases. Their visit to Silver City was coming to an end.

"I can't believe Mrs. Mason turned out to be the one causing all the mischief," Benny said as they walked down the hall. "I really thought the thirteenth floor was cursed. I kept thinking of all the years of bad luck we had ahead of us!"

"I knew we'd get to the bottom of it," Jessie said. "Now that we know what really happened, we don't need to worry about curses, broken mirrors, or the number thirteen."

Violet turned to look behind them. "How about black cats?" she asked. It seemed that Jinx had jumped down from her owner's lap and had silently followed them down the hall. Violet crouched. Jinx kneaded the carpet with her paws and purred. This time she was a little less shy. She even let Violet pet her ears.

The others crouched alongside Violet. Jinx showed off her fiercest hunting skills. She bent low, pounced on the rug, and batted at a piece of paper Henry had found in his pocket and made into a ball.

"Jinx doesn't bring anyone bad luck," Henry said with a grin. "Except maybe the mice."

Good Luck at the Bixby

About a month later, when school was out and summer had really begun, the children were out in the front yard. They were playing with their dog, Watch, when the mail carrier, Ms. Singleton, arrived.

"Another beautiful day in Greenfield!" Ms. Singleton said.

"And look," Benny said, pointing up. "This time there really isn't a cloud in the sky!"

"You're right about that," she said. From her sack, she took a fancy, cream-colored envelope and handed it to Benny. It was addressed to James and the Alden children. Benny tore open the envelope. Inside was an invitation to a party at the Bixby

Secret on the Thirteenth Floor

Building in Silver City.

Jessie read the fancy writing aloud. "'Join us for the Grand Opening of the Thirteenth Floor.'"

"Ooh, a party," said Ms. Singleton. "Make sure you take pictures!" She waved as she walked back to her white van.

The children ran inside and found Grandfather reading in his study. He checked the calendar and said the weekend was free. The Aldens were going back to Silver City, and this time it would be for a celebration!

The evening of the party, the children packed overnight bags for the trip and dressed in their best party clothes. Henry wore a navy sports coat and a blue tie. Benny chose a black dress shirt and a red bow tie from Grandfather's collection. Violet wore a purple dress, of course, and a pink beaded necklace, and Jessie wore a rainbow jumpsuit with a black belt. Grandfather looked handsome as always in white linen.

At six o'clock, the Aldens arrived at the Bixby. The stained glass windows in the front door sparkled in the setting sun. In the lobby, the enormous fireplace was no longer covered with plywood. Someone had restored the gray marble titles that surrounded the hearth, and the tile floor had been scrubbed and polished.

"You know," Benny said, pointing to the floor, "when I first saw the triangles in this pattern, I thought they looked like a monster's teeth, and it made me think the Bixby was spooky. But now that they are fixed up, I can see how much work it must have been to create this design. Now I don't think it's spooky—I think it's amazing!"

In the center of the wall, right above the fireplace, hung a gleaming brass horseshoe.

"I didn't notice that before either," Violet said.

"It's definitely new," Grandfather said. "Or maybe a 'new' antique. Hanging a horseshoe in your home is supposed to bring good luck, but only if you hang it this way, with the ends pointing up. If you hang a horseshoe upside down, people say the luck falls out."

"Thank goodness Gwen knew which way to hang it," Violet said. "Now she will have good luck for sure!"

"I love how Gwen has a sense of humor about everything she's been through," Grandfather said.

"I still don't believe in luck, whether it's good luck or bad luck," Jessie said. "But I am very happy that things have gotten better for Gwen."

When the elevator doors opened, Felix was inside.

"Well, hello there!" he said. Felix looked different wearing something other than his work overalls. He had on a striped tie, and he had trimmed his beard. "I just came from the basement," he said. "Everything is in tip-top shape."

"We can see that you've been working hard," Grandfather said. "The lobby has been completely restored."

"It's not just me," Felix said. "Everyone has pitched in. The workers, Gwen—even Mrs. Mason."

"Well, let's head up to the party!" Benny said.

"Thirteenth floor, coming right up," said Felix.

Henry looked at him in surprise. "You aren't worried about saying 'thirteen' anymore?"

Felix shook his head. "When we learned about the real cause of the fire, I realized that bad luck

had nothing to do with it. Since then, I've started to see things a little differently. Sometimes mirrors break, and as long as you clean up the glass, they can't hurt you. Same goes for the number thirteen. It's just a number."

The elevator doors opened on a party in full swing. The thirteenth floor looked beautiful. Not only had all the damage been repaired, but the careful work had preserved the quirky character of the building as well. All the old windows had been fixed and the tulip-shaped lights shined up. At the end of the hallway was an old piano. One of the tenants sat down and started to play. Some people started to dance. Others took a tour to admire what had changed about the Bixby and what would always stay the same.

"Hi, kids!" Gwen said. She gave them high fives and led them, along with Grandfather, into the apartment. It was impossible to tell that it had been so damaged by fire. Everything looked crisp and new.

Hayes stood next to the dining table, which was piled high with treats of all kinds—peanut butter cookies, brownies, blondies, caramel cupcakes, and, in the center, a giant chocolate layer cake.

Benny licked his lips. "Hayes, how did you know that chocolate cake was my favorite?"

Hayes shrugged. "I guess it's just a coincidence," he said.

Felix reached to take a peanut butter cookie and winked at Benny. "Some coincidences are good ones."

Turn the page to read a
sneak preview of

THE
POWER DOWN
MYSTERY

the next
Boxcar Children mystery!

The Aldens stood on the boardwalk and looked out over the harbor. Grandfather had brought the children to Port Elizabeth for the annual tall ships festival. But now the ships were sailing away.

Six-year-old Benny swung underneath the wooden railing at the edge of the marina. "Look at all the sails on that one!" he said. "Ten sails. No, eleven. Wait, twelve!"

At first, he had been sad the festival was ending early. But seeing the big boats in action was exciting. Colorful sails billowed on tall wooden masts. And the old-fashioned ships crashed through the waves.

In the marina, waves lapped onto the docks. With the tall ships gone, most of the docks were empty. On the ones that weren't, people scrambled about, getting ready to move newer, smaller boats.

Henry leaned his elbows on the railing next to Benny. Unlike his brother, Henry wasn't watching the ships. He was looking at the dark clouds chasing them away. At fourteen, Henry was the oldest of the Alden children, and he liked to pay attention to the weather. "The storm is coming in fast," he said. "I hope everyone gets to safety."

"The real storm isn't supposed to hit until later tonight," said Grandfather. "The ships will have plenty of time to find shelter up the coast."

"I'm glad we have people to forecast the weather," ten-year-old Violet said. "Imagine if we didn't have any warning before the storm."

Grandfather's friend Marie Freeman spoke up. "There are ships at the bottom of this harbor from the days when the sailors didn't get enough warning before storms hit." Ms. Freeman was the Aldens' host for the festival. She had lived in Port Elizabeth all her life. She loved to study old things.

"Even today, weather can be hard to predict," said Grandfather. "But it seems pretty likely that this storm will reach us before it dies out. I think the folks who run the festival made the right decision."

Benny was still more interested in the ships than the storm. As the children started walking toward the exit of the marina, he asked, "How do they know where to go? Once they get away from shore, all there is is waves! They don't even have street signs to follow! Don't they get lost?"

Ms. Freeman smiled. "I have a feeling those big, old ships might have some new technology onboard to tell them where they are. But sailors still have to know how to travel the old-fashioned way, just in case. What would they do if their computers failed?"

Benny stopped suddenly. "In the middle of the ocean? They'd never get home!"

"They would if they had the old tools and knew how to use them," Henry said. "We should try using a compass and map to find our way around."

"That sounds fun," Jessie said.

The Aldens came to the end of the marina. Violet noticed a line of smaller, newer-looking boats. Instead of sailing the boats away, people were loading them onto big trailers. On the dock next to the boats was a thin man in an orange raincoat. Around him were half a dozen people. They looked to be arguing with him.

"That's Hector Valencia," said Ms. Freeman. "He owns this marina. Poor guy. Ending the festival early can't be good for his business."

"Those people don't look happy with him," said Henry.

"I suppose everyone is trying to get their boats out of the water before the storm rolls in," said Grandfather. "But it looks like there's some sort of holdup."

"Looks like the boats are being inspected," Ms. Freeman said. "Unfortunately, there are rumors of smugglers here in Port Elizabeth."

Benny's eyes got big. "Smugglers? You mean like pirates?"

Ms. Freeman chuckled. "Not exactly. Smugglers are people who bring things in or out of the country illegally."

"What happens if they get caught?" Violet asked.

"It depends," said Ms. Freeman. "Say the smugglers brought in something that was legal to own, like jewels, but they snuck it in without paying taxes. They'd probably get a fine."

"That seems silly," said Jessie. "Why risk a fine

when you could be honest and not get in trouble?"

Ms. Freeman smiled. "That is a very good question. Sadly, not everyone is as sensible as you are. Most people are honest though. They just want to get their boats to safety."

Henry pointed at a large speedboat out in the bay. "I wonder whose boat that is," he said. The boat was anchored, and it didn't look like there was anyone aboard.

"I hope the owner hasn't forgotten about it," said Jessie. "If they don't move it and the storm hits, who knows what could happen to it?"

The empty boat bobbing on the dark water gave Benny a bad feeling. It reminded him of spooky stories he'd heard about ghost ships and pirates. He was happy when Ms. Freeman changed the subject.

"I'd like to check in on my shop before the storm hits," Ms. Freeman said. "Would you all mind if we stopped by?"

The Aldens agreed, and they followed Ms. Freeman into town. Along Main Street, they passed by empty gift shops and restaurants. Many were boarded up to protect against the coming storm.

The Happy Bear Ice-Cream Shop was just off Main Street. Outside the shop there was a tall statue of a smiling bear standing up on its back legs. The bear was wearing blue overalls and holding an ice-cream cone piled high with scoops.

"You didn't tell me us you had an ice-cream shop!" said Benny.

"I love your statue," said Violet. "It goes perfectly with the name of your shop."

"Why, thank you," said Ms. Freeman. "Bears became the symbol for our town a few years ago, and this fellow was made for my shop. I liked him so much, I changed the shop's name to match."

"So it's a town mascot?" Jessie asked.

"That's right," Ms. Freeman said. "The tourists like taking pictures with all the different bear statues around town."

A man in front of the shop next door gave a snort. "Maybe the storm will do everyone a favor and blow that one away."

"Why do you say that?" Henry asked.

The man stopped hammering and wiped his brow. He spoke with a strong southern accent.

"I believe this should be a high-class town with high-class shops. People see that silly bear and the silly name and think they can bring their drippity ice cream anyplace." He frowned at the children. "Kids come into my shop and let it drip all over. Then they touch things with their sticky hands."

The man turned back to his work. "At least my shop will be protected from this coming storm," he said.

Once the Aldens were in the ice-cream shop, Violet whispered, "That man didn't seem very nice."

Ms. Freeman sighed. "That is George Williams. He's not really so bad. He just moved here from Georgia. He doesn't understand Port Elizabeth yet. If he had it his way, there'd only be fancy gift shops like his."

"Why does he want you to change your shop's name?" asked Jessie.

"Yeah, I like The Happy Bear," said Benny. "It's... happy!"

Ms. Freeman gave a small smile. "My shop used to be called Sailor's Delight Sweets and Treats. It went along with the name of the shop next door, The Stylish Sailor Boutique. But a couple years ago, I decided to just sell ice cream and changed the name. He's always trying to get me to go back to selling fancy candies and knickknacks."

"Well, I think ice cream is the perfect thing to sell," said Benny. "Shoppers need energy. They can take a break with ice cream and have more energy to shop."

"I'll bet you're right," Ms. Freeman said. "How about some energy for you kids? Give your orders to Savannah."

The young woman behind the counter had not looked up from her cell phone since the Aldens entered the shop.

Ms. Freeman sighed. "Savannah!"

The young woman jumped and looked up. She had long, brown hair and wore a purple shirt.

"Take the Aldens' orders, please," Ms. Freeman said. "I'm going to check on the generator."

As the woman rang them up, Violet said, "I like your shirt. Purple is my favorite color. Your bracelets and earrings are nice too. Are the red stones rubies? And pearls?"

The young woman blushed. "Oh, these? They aren't anything special. Only stuff I put together." She turned away to scoop ice cream. Violet wanted to ask about her name tag, which said *Sarah* instead of Savannah. But it did not seem like the woman wanted to talk.

The children and Grandfather sat at a table and ate their ice cream. Soon Ms. Freeman joined them.

Henry asked, "Are you worried about the storm, Ms. Freeman? Should we put up boards like the man next door?"

"I've seen enough storms hit Port Elizabeth," Ms. Freeman said. "We'll survive one more. I'm only concerned about one thing. We've had some issues with the power lately. It's the strangest thing. Some days I come in, and the ice cream is soft and runny—like it's been melting overnight."

"That is strange," Henry said.

"I have a backup generator though," Ms. Freeman continued. "So if the power does go out, the generator will turn on. It will keep the ice cream cold and run the security system."

Benny's eyes got wide. "Security system? Do you think someone will come and steal the ice cream?"

Ms. Freeman smiled. "More likely they'd steal money from the cash register. We don't keep much overnight, but it's better to be safe. Things can get a little crazy when a storm hits. You never know what people will do."

"Maybe we should stay here and protect the ice cream," said Benny. "Just in case."

Everyone laughed. "We'll be more comfortable at Ms. Freeman's house," said Grandfather. He winked at Benny. "We can get some ice cream to go, for after dinner."

Benny nodded. "That's a good idea. And after the storm, we'll come back and make sure the ice cream is safe."

Add to Your Boxcar Children Collection with New Books and Sets!

The first twelve books are now available in three individual boxed sets!

978-0-8075-0854-1 · US $24.99

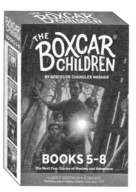

978-0-8075-0857-2 · US $24.99

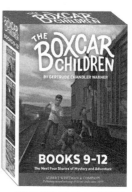

978-0-8075-0840-4 · US $24.99

The Boxcar Children Bookshelf includes the first twelve books, a bookmark with complete title checklist, and a poster with activities.

978-0-8075-0855-8 · US $69.99

The Boxcar Children 20-Book Set includes Gertrude
Chandler Warner's original nineteen books,
plus an all-new activity book, stickers,
and a magnifying glass!

978-0-8075-0847-3 · US $132.81

THE BOXCAR CHILDREN

GREAT ADVENTURE

An Exciting 5-Book Miniseries

**Henry, Jessie, Violet, and Benny Alden
are on a secret mission that takes
them around the world!**

When Violet finds a turtle statue that nobody's seen
before in an old trunk at home, the children are on the
case! The clue turns out to be an invitation to the
Reddimus Society, a secret guild dedicated to returning
lost treasures to where they belong.

Now the Aldens must take the statue and six mysterious
boxes across the country to deliver them safely—and keep
them out of the hands of the Reddimus Society's enemies.
It's just the beginning of
the Boxcar Children's
most amazing
adventure yet!

HC 978-0-8075-0695-0
PB 978-0-8075-0696-7

HC 978-0-8075-0698-1
PB 978-0-8075-0699-8

HC 978-0-8075-0684-4
PB 978-0-8075-0685-1

HC 978-0-8075-0687-5
PB 978-0-8075-0688-2

HC 978-0-8075-0681-3
PB 978-0-8075-0682-0

Also available as a boxed set!
978-0-8075-0693-6 · $34.95

Hardcover US $12.99 · Paperback US $6.99

Introducing The Boxcar Children Early Readers!

Adapted from the beloved chapter books, these new early readers allow kids to begin reading with the stories that started it all.

HC 978-0-8075-0839-8 · US $12.99
PB 978-0-8075-0835-0 · US $3.99

HC 978-0-8075-7675-5 · US $12.99
PB 978-0-8075-7679-3 · US $3.99

HC 978-0-8075-9367-7 · US $12.99
PB 978-0-8075-9370-7 · US $3.99

HC 978-0-8075-5402-9 · US $12.99
PB 978-0-8075-5435-7 · US $3.99

978-0-8075-2850-1 · US $6.99

Introducing Interactive Mysteries!

Have you ever wanted to help the Aldens crack a case? Now you can with this interactive, choose-your-path-style mystery!

The Boxcar Children, Fully Illustrated!

This fully illustrated edition celebrates Gertrude Chandler Warner's timeless story. Featuring all-new full-color artwork as well as an afterword about the author, the history of the book, and the Boxcar Children legacy, this volume will be treasured by first-time readers and longtime fans alike.

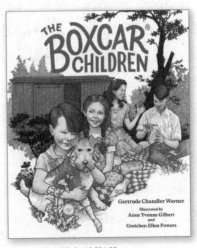

978-0-8075-0925-8 · US $34.99

GERTRUDE CHANDLER WARNER discovered when she was teaching that many readers who like an exciting story could find no books that were both easy and fun to read. She decided to try to meet this need, and her first book, *The Boxcar Children*, quickly proved she had succeeded.

Miss Warner drew on her own experiences to write the mystery. As a child she spent hours watching trains go by on the tracks opposite her family home. She often dreamed about what it would be like to set up housekeeping in a caboose or freight car—the situation the Alden children find themselves in.

While the mystery element is central to each of Miss Warner's books, she never thought of them as strictly juvenile mysteries. She liked to stress the Aldens' independence and resourcefulness and their solid New England devotion to using up and making do. The Aldens go about most of their adventures with as little adult supervision as possible—something else that delights young readers.

Miss Warner lived in Putnam, Connecticut, until her death in 1979. During her lifetime, she received hundreds of letters from girls and boys telling her how much they liked her books.

31901065031785